About the author

The ideas for *The Naturals* came to author Sharon Petersen over several years, and she grasped any opportunity to write while her five children were small. She lived in Denmark for 11 years, returning to the UK when her husband died. She and her children now live in Hampshire.

The Naturals

Sharon R. C. Petersen

illustrated by

Georgina M Walton

Book Guild Publishing

Sussex, England

First published in Great Britain in 2010 by
The Book Guild Ltd
Pavilion View
19 New Road
Brighton, BN1 1UF

Printed in Thailand under the supervision of
MRM Graphics Ltd, Winslow, Bucks

A catalogue record for this book is available from
The British Library.

ISBN 978 1 84624 340 0

Contents

Foreword

My passion behind writing *The Naturals* is to try and help fuel
a sense of wonder within children at the very real connection
we have with our natural world around us, so that they may feel
inspired to revere, respect and protect it.

I hope to show that not only is our natural world alive and
compassionate, but that it has our best interests at heart at all
times, and throughout my stories I hope the sound moral values
within *The Naturals* shine through.

A percentage of my profits from *The Naturals* will be going to the
WWT to help save wetlands for wildlife and people; and also to
the NSPCC to help stop child abuse.

Thank you for reading my stories to the children in your life.

Sharon R. C. Petersen

www.thenaturals.uk.com

We do not inherit the Earth from our ancestors;
we borrow it from our children.
(Native American Proverb)

This is The Story of

Cloudy

How can small Cloudy
possibly help baby Eagle
in her distress?

The Naturals

Once upon a time a baby eagle lived with her mother, in a nest perched right at the top of a really tall tree. Baby Eagle adored living in their high perch, which was far from the dangers lurking nearer the ground. Their tree was the tallest tree in the whole forest, or so Baby Eagle thought. She would peek her beak out of the nest and, standing on tiptoes, she could just about see the tops of the neighbouring trees far below.

Whilst her mother was away hunting for food, Baby Eagle passed the time looking at the wonderfully open sky. With wings outstretched, she tried touching Cloudies with her wing tip as they floated nearby. Baby Eagle would shout out 'Hello' to the Cloudies, and ask them which shape they were that day – or just try and guess!

Now, there was one particular Cloudy who was very happy drifting wherever Windy fancied blowing him each day. Cloudy's favourite game in the whole world was to try and shape himself into whatever he could see on big Earth below. Sometimes it would be a horse, or a tractor, or a tree … or maybe a hippopotamus! Cloudy had even once managed to turn himself into a snowman!

The Naturals

One day Cloudy happened to have been blown apart from the other Cloudies in the sky, but he thought it was nice to be all alone and able to look far out to the horizon as normally his view was obscured by other Cloudies. Windy wasn't particularly strong that day and Cloudy was enjoying the chance to hover over a spot of land. Usually Cloudy only just had time to change shape before Windy would push him along to a change of scenery, and then he would have to change shape all over again!

Meanwhile, Mother Eagle kissed her baby goodbye and promised to return soon with some food. The eaglet snuggled down inside her cosy nest, enjoying having it all to herself. She was twittering away as she looked up at the blue sky above, and at Sunny, and daydreaming of the day when she could soar away from the nest.

After a while, Baby Eagle began to get all hot and sweaty, and wished her mother would return so she could hide underneath her wings, and be shielded from Sunny's warm sunshine rays, like she normally was.

The Story of Cloudy

Cloudy was passing slowly along when he caught sight of Baby Eagle trying to stretch her wings to shield herself from Sunny's warm light. He wondered where her mother was, because Sunny's rays were getting hotter and hotter …

But there was no sign of her mother, and Baby Eagle crouched down inside the nest to wait patiently. The top of her head began to get extremely hot and so she tucked her head tight under her wing. After a while her wing became too hot so she switched to her other wing … then she lay down on her back, but her tummy became too hot, so she lifted both her legs into the air and spread her talons. She pretended her legs were trees and her talons branches, and she tried to scrunch herself up underneath!

She remembered that when she normally got herself into this position, it was to *warm* her feet by Sunny, and let Sunny tickle her talons. Now, though, her feet had already become far too hot!

Little Eagle then noticed a small, white, fluffy Cloudy high up in the sky, and wished that it was in front of Sunny so she could have some shade. Then she said aloud, 'Well, that little Cloudy is too small anyway. Just move along now, Cloudy, and make way for some bigger Cloudies, please!'

The little Cloudy could not hear her, but he did think she was looking more and more uncomfortable, perched high in the nest without shade. He decided that help was needed, and looked all around for some big Cloudies. Although there were some on the far horizon, they were too far away to be of any use …

Then little Cloudy had an idea: if he could just become a big, dark Cloudy filled with Rainy, he would then persuade Windy to blow him above Baby Eagle's nest, and be her protection from Sunny's rays until her mother returned! He studied Earth below and immediately spotted what looked like a large puddle of water. 'That'll do perfectly!' little Cloudy said with glee. 'Now I just need Windy to nudge me left a bit, then I can suck up some water and turn myself into a Rainy Cloudy, with Sunny's help, of course. Blow me please Windy … blow … blow!' And Windy blew …

With his eyes on Baby Eagle, Cloudy wished with all his might for Sunny to evaporate lots of water from the large puddle underneath to fill him up. Baby Eagle was wriggling around uncomfortably in her nest. Cloudy wished and wished, and then wished some more. He shouted out loud to Sunny for her help.

As Sunny sat smiling in the sky, she heard Cloudy's pleas and felt his strong desire to help Baby Eagle, and, of course, she helped. Even though her strong rays were too hot for the little bird, they needed to be strong to evaporate water for little Cloudy to hold, which would in turn help Baby Eagle.

Little Cloudy had never managed to become a proper Rainy Cloudy before. He had always felt too small to be of any help. He couldn't even give the flowers a good drink because he had only ever previously managed to drizzle, and not pour down.

Right now, though, Cloudy was beginning to feel heavier, and he was looking darker. With his eye still on Baby Eagle, he kept wishing extremely hard to be as full as he could be. He was feeling excited and nervous at the same time. He was nervous because time was of the essence, and excited at the thought of spitting down whopping big Rainy drops, instead of only squirting drizzle. Most importantly, he would be helping someone in need!

When Cloudy was bigger than he ever imagined he could be, and he felt heavy enough to burst, he whistled to Windy to blow and blow again, to push him into just the right position to help Baby Eagle.

Windy was very helpful and blew and blew. 'But you must blow more, dear Windy!' shouted Cloudy, 'I am the biggest and heaviest I have ever been. You need more puff – and quickly!' So Windy huffed and puffed, and blew little Cloudy, who was not so little any more, towards the eaglet's nest.

By this time Baby Eagle was so hot she didn't know what to do with herself. She was running round and round in circles in the nest, which, of course, was making her even hotter!

'Nearly there!' shouted Cloudy to Windy. 'I'm coming, Baby Eagle … I'm coming!' Cloudy called over to the little bird. Baby Eagle stopped running around her nest because she thought she heard Windy howling and whistling above her. She looked up, and could not believe her eyes when she saw the only Cloudy in a clear blue sky beginning to cover Sunny!

'Where on Earth did you spring from, Cloudy?" she asked. "You couldn't be that little squirt of a Cloudy I saw before! Oh, what a relief to be in the shade!'

But Cloudy hadn't finished helping yet! He then squeezed and squashed himself together to squirt Rainy out. However, it wasn't a Rainy *squirt* that landed on Baby Eagle's head, but more like a *waterfall*! 'Whoops! Sorry, little bird,' whistled Cloudy, whilst Baby Eagle coughed and spluttered under the drenching!

The Story of Cloudy

'That's okay, I don't mind at all, Cloudy!' replied Baby Eagle.

By now, Baby Eagle was splashing around, feather-deep in rainwater, cooling down nicely and loving every second! But then she got a little concerned. 'Perhaps you'd better stop now, Cloudy, before Rainy washes my nest away!' she shouted.

Cloudy somehow managed to stop his flow of water to barely a drizzle, and Baby Eagle's new 'swimming pool' started to seep away through the nest. She had so enjoyed her first swim, but now that she was wet through, standing in the shade of Cloudy, well … Baby Eagle had begun to feel a little chilly!

So with Windy's help, Cloudy moved aside, allowing Sunny's warmth to envelop Baby Eagle once more. This time, however, it was simply for the little bird's pleasure! She was beginning to warm up just nicely. Her feathers were looking all fluffy and puffy, and the nest was drying out and looking like new. She then caught a glimpse of her mother in the distance, flying home.

'Hello Baby! I'm sorry it took so long for me to hunt for food today, but I'm back now. Have you been all right all by yourself?' asked Mother Eagle, worried.

'Oh, don't worry about me, Mother, I've been *well* taken care of!' Baby Eagle looked towards the sky at Sunny, and at the half-filled Rainy Cloudy who was happily dropping his drizzle over some thirsty flowers in the distance ...

... And as Sunny kisses Moony goodnight with her reflection, Moony says, 'Have a safe and peaceful day, Sunny,' to which Sunny replies, 'Have a safe and peaceful night, Moony.' And all the twinkling Starries glitter and giggle, 'Goodnight ... goodnight.'

Cloudy

Was Baby Eagle right to judge Cloudy just by looking at his size? Do you think he has now learnt that size doesn't matter?

Was Cloudy pleased this important job came his way, do you think?

Could Cloudy have chosen to ignore Baby Eagle's plight ~ and had a nice relaxing day, leisurely drifting on by?

I wonder if Baby Eagle now knows not to judge ~ and trusts that Cloudy will always look after her?

This is The Story of

Snowy

Does Snowy really have
to turn little Foxy into a
freezing statue to save him?

O*nce* upon a time there lived a mischievous little fox cub. He was forever getting into trouble inside his cosy den, where he lived with his mother, father and two sisters, Fauna and Flo.

'Come away from the entrance, Foxy,' his mother warned more than once. 'Father will be back in a minute with food in his mouth, and he'll trip right over you!'

'No he won't, Mother. I'm keeping a lookout, and I'll spot him first, I promise!' Foxy replied, and then asked, 'Why can't *I* go hunting with Father, anyhow? When will I be allowed to go and explore the world outside the den, Mother? When, Mother, when?'

'Hush now, Foxy – you must have patience,' explained Foxy's mother, 'There is no rush, for you must learn all you can inside the den first. Come and snuggle up with your sisters and me now.'

'Oh, Mother, do I have to? It's much more fun over here looking out the doorway, waiting for Father to come home!'

'Yes, Foxy, you have to,' said Mother patiently. 'You may not think you are chilly, but you are still small and we need to snuggle up together.'

'But I don't like snuggling!' whined Foxy.

'That is quite enough, Foxy!' Mother exclaimed, not so patiently. 'Come over here, please.'

Foxy finally gave in and went and snuggled up to his mother and sisters.

Time went by in those early weeks, albeit a little too slowly for Foxy's liking, living snugly in the den that was home to him and his family. He grew more and more restless cooped up inside, but finally the day came when Foxy's parents decided it was time to take their three cubs for a little exploration outside the den.

'At last … finally!' whooped Foxy with great joy.

'You will be with us, won't you, Mother?' asked Foxy's sisters anxiously. 'You won't lose us, will you, Father?'

'No, no, no! Of course not, little ones,' chuckled Father. 'Mother and I will be right with you all. We won't let you out of our sight, will we, Mother?'

'Absolutely not, darlings!' replied Mother.

'What, not even for half an hour?' piped up Foxy rather cheekily.

'Not even for half a second!' exclaimed Mother.

The Story of Snowy

'That's boring,' stated Foxy. 'I want to go exploring all on my own!'

'You'll stay with your mother and me or you'll not be stepping one paw outside of this den, do you understand, little Foxy?' Father told Foxy sternly.

'Yes, yes, message understood, Father, sorry …' Foxy mumbled lamely.

So, bright and early the next morning, Foxy and his family were ready to set off on the cubs' first adventurous steps outdoors. Mischievous Foxy was so excited that he could hardly contain himself. That some very wonderful things were bound to happen, the little fox cub was certain.

Out of the den they all stepped, into the chill of the air and the bright light of Sunny. The fox cubs had to blink many times in the sunlight, but they were soon staring in wonderment at the white blanket covering everything in sight.

'Oh, how exciting! She must have fallen during the night,' observed Mother.

'Who has fallen during the night, Mother? What is it?' asked Foxy, puzzled.

'Snowy, dear!' replied Mother. 'Snowy has fallen. Maybe we should postpone our day outside until Sunny has melted Snowy, otherwise your little paws will get very cold walking on Snowy!'

'That's not a problem!' shouted Foxy. 'We can't leave Snowy now. Just look at her … she's so beautiful! All white and soft and crunchy.'

'And *cold*!' chorused Fauna and Flo who, Foxy impatiently observed, were already huddling together – even when they didn't have to! They were more than happy standing by the den, and there they would gladly have stayed. Foxy, however, had other ideas, ideas that certainly did not include hanging around the boring den!

'Sunny's out, and it's warm enough for Snowy to soon melt – I think we can carry on,' Father suggested.

'Very sensible, Father! Good idea!' agreed Foxy readily. 'Let's get going! Over here, this way …'

'We're coming, Foxy!' Fauna and Flo shouted. 'Wait for us!'

'Slow down there, Foxy!' shouted Father. 'We can't lose you on your first trip outside. You'd never find your way back to the den again – and that wouldn't do at all – would it, Mother?'

Foxy did not listen to Mother's response. 'Oh yes, I *would* find my way!' he was busily mumbling to himself, and he carried on eagerly, as if he hadn't heard Father's words at all.

'Flo, Fauna, look over here!' Foxy yelled to his sisters. He had stopped in his tracks and was looking intently at something through the bushes. His sisters caught up with him and watched in wonder at a big pond, buzzing with life all around. Their gazes went from the dragonflies humming over it and the kingfishers diving into it, to the otters swimming under it and the insects and ducks sitting on it.

'Go ahead and have a drink from the pond, cubs,' said Mother.

'But we shouldn't!' whispered Foxy.

'Why ever not, Foxy?' asked Father.

'Because we'll disturb everyone!' Foxy remarked anxiously.

'Dearest Foxy,' chuckled Mother, 'how very thoughtful you are! But you are a part of "everyone" and you too may drink from the pond. Besides, if you all go *quietly* to the water's edge, you will not disturb *anyone*.

So they did just that. With tails curled under their bodies and snouts near the ground, Fauna and Flo followed Foxy to the water's edge. Unfortunately they were following each other a little too closely, and when Foxy stopped, Fauna and Flo did not! This resulted in Fauna's snout bumping into Foxy's bottom, and Flo's snout bumping into Fauna's bottom! Foxy could not believe it when he found himself being pushed head-first into the pond!

'SPLASH! SPLOSH!' went the once calm water. The dragonflies hummed away. The ducks flew away. The otters swam away. However, the insects remained.

The Naturals

'I can't believe that just happened!' declared Foxy when he surfaced. He then scrambled back up the bank, complaining, 'Now we've disturbed *everyone*!'

'Sorry, Foxy, we're really sorry,' mumbled his sisters, rather ashamed.

I really need to be on my own, thought Foxy to himself. *I'm ready to explore this world and I'm getting nowhere with my family on my tail!* So he decided that he would wander off for just a little while. 'Yes, that's what I'll do!' Foxy said out loud to himself. 'I'll run round the pond – that won't take too long. Mother and Father won't even have time to miss me!' And off he ran without another thought …

Foxy noticed that he was making paw prints in Snowy, and he had an idea … if he did get lost following the pond, then he would just follow his own paw prints back again! 'Brilliant idea, you're a genius!' he marvelled to himself. But Foxy didn't realise that Sunny was already melting the top layer of Snowy, so that his paw prints were soon disappearing …

The Story of Snowy

The Naturals

Foxy felt a pang of doubt tickling inside his tummy, which reminded him that he was all alone. However, he pushed that thought out of his mind and carried on following the pond, although now he ran a bit quicker!

After a while, whilst Fauna and Flo were scrambling around in Snowy together, Mother called, 'Come along now cubs, let's head back to our cosy den. I think that's enough excitement for a first outing!'

'Coming, Mother!' called Flo and Fauna. 'Here we are!'

'Good girls,' said Mother. 'Now, where's your brother? Foxy! Where are you?' she called.

'Foxy, come over here!' Father called loudly, to no avail.

'We haven't seen him for quite a while,' offered Fauna.

'Oh no! He's wandered off! We've lost him,' cried Mother.

'I'll search for him, Mother dear,' comforted Father. 'Don't worry, our Foxy's smart, he'll be back.' And with that, he leapt off into the Snowy distance, calling for Foxy.

Mother Fox led Fauna and Flo back to their den to await Father's return with Foxy.

Foxy's heart was beating excitedly, even though his head was telling him he should turn back. He had never in his life felt such freedom and responsibility all at once. *This pond seems bigger than I thought*, he realised, getting a bit annoyed. He decided to run a bit faster …

Foxy was so intent on making it all round the pond that he didn't notice Sunny starting to disappear behind the trees. He knew that if he turned back now, he would be told off by Mother and Father, and would probably not be allowed out of the den for years and years! However, if he continued following the pond and found his own way home again, his mother and father would be *very* proud of him, and would realise that Foxy was, indeed, old enough to explore the world alone! At least this is what Foxy thought – he ran faster still …

Meanwhile, Father was quietly concentrating on which direction to take. He sniffed the air and he sniffed the ground, and his eyes searched all around. He had a feeling that Foxy might try to run all round the pond, but what Foxy didn't know was how huge the pond was, and that it would take hours and hours to run round it.

Father could find no trace of paw prints in Snowy. 'That's not very helpful of you, Snowy. At a time like this I could have done with some paw-print help,' Father said aloud. Then he realised it was actually Sunny who had melted away Foxy's paw prints. 'That's not very helpful of you, Sunny,' he muttered, before remembering that Sunny was keeping his little Foxy warm on this Snowy day.

Foxy was beginning to get a little bit worried, *and* a bit cold. He hadn't ever felt cold before because Mother was always making him snuggle up with her and his sisters. For a split second, Foxy wanted to be snuggled up with Mother!

Foxy realised that when he ran really fast he didn't feel so cold, so he ran really fast. But when he ran really fast, he felt really tired, *and* he felt really hungry. All of a sudden, Foxy stopped. He realised this wasn't fun and exciting anymore. He wanted to be inside his cosy den. He wanted his mother. He even wanted to snuggle!

Foxy decided to turn back. He had had enough freedom and responsibility for now. But just as he was about to head back the way he had come, he sensed something he had never felt before – he sensed danger!

Foxy was frightened, although he didn't understand why, exactly. His ears were stretching up and his tail was stretching out, and he stood as still as a statue. Foxy was too scared to move an inch. In fact, he couldn't even try. He was literally frozen with fear – and getting colder by the second.

Poor Foxy noticed Snowy fluttering big cotton wool balls from the sky which stuck on to his fur. *I thought you were so great this morning, Snowy,* Foxy miserably thought to himself, *but now you are just making things worse for me.*

Snowy carried on silently falling onto Foxy. She knew what was best for Foxy, even though Foxy may not realise it for a very long time. She knew it was for his own protection that little Foxy should stay as still as a statue, for as long as possible, as danger was, indeed, lurking close by, in the form of large forest animals.

Foxy stayed as still as possible because, as well as being frightened stiff, he was by now *frozen* stiff too!

Father was finding it more and more difficult to walk, let alone run, through the thickening Snowy. 'Snowy, please stop!' Father shouted out loud. 'And help me find my Foxy!' Snowy fluttered silently down, seemingly ignoring Father's pleas. She was intent on the most important job, which was protecting little Foxy from imminent danger.

The forest became dark and Foxy closed his eyes. He forgot all about his hunger and his fear, and he didn't seem to feel the cold anymore, even though he was covered with Snowy! *That's better*, thought Snowy, *a nice Snowy blanket covering!* Snowy was very pleased with herself!

Father grumbled, 'I'll find Foxy first thing in the morning – *without* your help, Snowy!' And with that, he settled down to rest for the night.

The Story of Snowy

Snowy didn't seem to mind Father's words. She blanketed herself around the cosy den that Father had found to rest in, so that he would be warm enough through the night. She made sure little Foxy was as still as could be throughout the entire night. He was by now cold and hard, but with a thick protective covering of Snowy, so he didn't freeze solid.

First thing the next morning, as soon as Snowy knew that little Foxy was no longer in any close danger from the larger forest animals, she called to Sunny to wake up. 'You have lots of work to do this morning, Sunny. Will you please melt all my hard work from last night?'

'Of course I will, dear Snowy. Oh what fun, making everything warm and dry once again!' enthused Sunny.

So Sunny heated, and Snowy melted, Father awoke, and Foxy blinked. Father leapt from his resting place to continue his search. Foxy still could not move. He didn't sense danger any more, but he was numb with being so cold!

The Naturals

Snowy had all but disappeared, although she was watching from a distance, making sure that Foxy was found safely by his father. Sure enough, after a while, Father spotted up ahead an odd-looking little Foxy with ears stretched up and tail stretched out. He ran over to him. 'Foxy! Foxy! Am I glad to see you! What a naughty thing to do, running away like that!' he scolded him, but then felt concerned. 'You look like a statue, son! Are you all right?'

The Story of Snowy

'Oh, Father! I'm *so* pleased to see you – and I'm *very* sorry! I'll *never* run off again! And Father, I *feel* like a statue!' little Foxy said, explaining. 'It was that unhelpful Snowy, falling all over me all night long.'

'I know, son. Snowy stopped me from finding you last night,' complained Father. 'I had to stop for the night and find shelter. Still, she's all gone now, thank goodness. Let's just get you thawed out and back to the den, where you belong.'

'Oh, yes, *please*,' begged little Foxy.

It wasn't long before Sunny had brought all the feeling back into Foxy's little body, and father and son could walk back home. With Foxy's ears now drooping backwards, and with his tail between his legs, he arrived at his cosy den to face a good telling off from his dear mother, who was waiting outside.

Mother Fox was happy and angry, all at the same time. After a big hug she said, 'And what have you got to say for yourself, Foxy?'

Little Foxy, with his tail still between his legs, had just opened his mouth to speak, when Fauna and Flo came flying out of the den, jumped on top of Foxy and shouted, 'Foxy! Foxy! You're back! You're back!' When they got off of him, Mother repeated, 'Well, Foxy, I'm waiting for an answer.'

'Mother,' replied Foxy, 'apart from saying, I'm so sorry and I promise it will *never* happen again, I would just like to ask one thing … can we all have a snuggle?' And with that, he ran into the den, with Flo and Fauna following closely behind.

'Well, Father dear, maybe, just *maybe* our Foxy's learnt a good lesson out of this experience,' said Mother hopefully.

'Well, *I* certainly have where that Snowy's concerned!' said Father.

'Oh yes!' gushed Mother. 'Without Snowy looking after our little Foxy last night, who knows *what* dangers he would have faced!'

The Story of Snowy

'Well, I … er … I suppose you're *right*, Mother!' pondered Father, as they followed their children inside the den.

'There is just one more thing, Foxy,' said Mother. 'As your punishment, you will not set one paw outside this den for weeks and weeks!'

'Oh, Mother!' cried Foxy. 'Please, can it not be for *years* and *years*?!'

Foxy and his family all laughed and snuggled up together inside their cosy den, daydreaming about what other scary and exciting adventures were in store for them in the future …

... And as Sunny kisses Moony goodnight with her reflection, Moony says, 'Have a safe and peaceful day, Sunny,' to which Sunny replies, 'Have a safe and peaceful night, Moony.' And all the twinkling Starries glitter and giggle, 'Goodnight … goodnight.'

Snowy

Could Foxy understand Snowy was helping him,
or could he only see that Snowy
was making him cold?

Did Snowy like making Foxy cold or was she only
interested in saving him, do you think?

When Mother fox told Father that Snowy had
helped their son, did she also help him to realise
that there is always another way
to look at things?

This is The Story of

Windy

Can it be true that Windy
may not be so mean
after all?

The Naturals

Once upon a time there was a boy called Tom who lived with his little sister, Katie, and with Mummy and Daddy, in a house by the park. Nearly every day either Mummy or Daddy would take them to play in the park, and sometimes they would all go together. When only Mummy took them, they had to do their cardigan buttons right up so that Windy didn't blow a chill onto their tummies. When only Daddy took them, he would say, 'Never mind about a cardigan, we'll run away from Windy as fast as we can and that will keep us warm!'

There was a time when Windy blew so hard that he blew little Katie up into the air and she landed on her bottom – even though Daddy was holding her hand! Daddy said it was lucky Windy did that, otherwise Katie would have trodden in a big dollop of dog poo that Daddy hadn't seen! Tom didn't think it was lucky – he thought Windy was being mean, and was actually trying to blow his little sister right *into* the dog poo!

The Story of Windy

The Naturals

Another time when Windy blew hard, Tom saw an
old lady running after her umbrella that was blowing
away. She chased it right to the top of the road before she
caught it, and then hopped on to a bus. Tom told
Mummy it was mean of Windy to make the lady
run like that. Mummy said it was quite lucky
really, otherwise she would have missed
her bus. Tom wasn't so sure about that.

The Story of Windy

One day Tom was having fun in the park with Windy. He and Katie were chasing leaves that were being blown off the trees and blowing around and around in the park. Tom was just thinking that *maybe* Windy wasn't *always* mean, because they *were* having such fun, when he noticed a single leaf with beautiful colours hanging from the branch of a tree and flapping around. It was the only leaf left on the whole tree, and then, in an instant, it was gone, having been blown away by Windy!

Tom decided then that Windy was, in fact, a *meany* Windy, to blow all the leaves off a poor tree who was just standing there looking beautiful one minute, and naked and cold the next. Well, that was just mean, thought Tom. Mummy did suggest that the leaves were now put to good use on the ground, being a blanket for the worms and insects and sleeping plant roots, but Tom was too busy playing a stamping-on-the-leaves game to notice the many living things underneath.

It was soon to be Katie's birthday. Tom wished that it was his birthday too, because he had such a long time to wait until he was nine, although Katie, of course, had to wait four long years until she reached that age! Tom was glad that he would be nine first. He liked being older than Katie. Sometimes he didn't like having a little sister, although he really *did* like being an older brother!

Every morning for a week before Katie's birthday, Mummy reminded Tom to draw a birthday card for his sister, and every evening when Mummy was tucking Tom into bed, she asked if he had drawn one yet. Tom would say, 'Oh oh! No … but I'll do it tomorrow!' And so it went on until the morning of Katie's birthday, when he *still* had not drawn a card. Instead, Mummy let Tom write his name on Katie's card from Mummy and Daddy. Mummy was not very pleased with Tom, and Tom did feel a little bit guilty. But Katie didn't seem bothered that Tom hadn't drawn her a birthday card, and he told himself that because Katie didn't know that he *should* have made her one, it really didn't seem to matter so much.

For a birthday treat, Mummy, Daddy, Katie and Tom were going to the funfair. Tom was really excited, as he could pretend that it was his birthday too! Plus he would have more fun than Katie because he and Mummy would go on all the big exciting rides, whilst Daddy took Katie on the 'baby' rides. Daddy said that he didn't like to go on rides that tickled his tummy and made his face green! Tom thought a ride like that sounded *great* fun! He wouldn't mind having a green painted face!

It was nearly dark when they arrived at the funfair, and everyone was excited. Daddy gave Tom two pounds for popcorn and drink. Mummy mentioned to Tom that he might like to spend a little bit on something for Katie, as he hadn't drawn her a card. Tom gave her one piece of popcorn and, as she seemed happy with that, he ate all the rest himself! He didn't feel too guilty about that either …

The big Ferris wheel was all lit up and looking so pretty, and so high, that Tom couldn't resist asking Mummy if they could have a go. Mummy asked Tom if he was certain, because it looked quite scary – even for Mummy! Tom said yes, he was certain, and so they joined the queue.

Once they were in their own carriage and starting to move, Tom was all excited.

'Just wait until we reach the top, Tom!' said Mummy. 'That's the scariest bit, so don't go rocking the carriage then, will you?'

'What, Mummy — like this, do you mean?' said Tom, daringly rocking the carriage forwards and backwards, forwards and backwards …

'Yes, that's what I mean Tom, and I don't think you'll like it so much when we're right up high in the sky!'

'Oh, yes I will!' exclaimed Tom, 'I'll *love* it!'

They slowly moved up higher and higher. Tom continued to rock the carriage a little bit, just to show Mummy that he wasn't scared, even though it made his tummy tickle quite a lot!

The further they climbed away from the noise and lights of the fair, the darker and quieter it became. Tom was glad he had Mummy right next to him, holding him tight. 'If you're scared, Mummy, you can just hold me tight!' said Tom, not wanting Mummy to realise that it was *he* who really wanted to hold on tight to Mummy!

'Thank you, Tom — I'm okay, but could you stop rocking the carriage now, please?' said Mummy.

'I'm *not* rocking it, Mummy – I thought *you* were!' declared Tom.

'Oh, sorry Tom! It must just be Windy having a bit of fun with us!' said Mummy.

'Well, that's not a nice thing to do, Windy!' said Tom loudly into the dusky sky. 'Stop that blowing, Windy!'

Mummy laughed. 'Don't worry, Tom, you can't control Windy, and there's no use in trying! Let's just sit back and enjoy the ride.'

'But Windy's just being mean again! I don't *want* the carriage to rock!' Tom said, getting a bit alarmed.

'Calm down, Tom, Mummy's here,' she soothed. 'Hold on tight to me, and we'll soon be on the ground again.'

When the Ferris wheel finally stopped spinning, Tom couldn't wait to get off and ran straight into Daddy's arms. 'That mean Windy followed me here and purposely tried to tip Mummy and me out of the Ferris wheel!' he cried.

'There, there, Tom,' said Daddy. 'I'm sure Windy was just trying to be helpful, and only wanted to make it more fun for you. After all, you *did* say you liked it when the carriage rocked.'

'Well, yes, but Windy shouldn't interfere! She made my tummy tickle *too* much,' complained Tom.

'And gave you a bit of a green face too, by the looks of it, Tom!' Daddy pointed out.

While Tom was thinking about how he had managed to get a green face when it hadn't even been painted, Katie was yelling that it was time to move on, and pulled Daddy and Mummy towards the merry-go-round.

After they had been on many rides, and had wandered round looking at all the funfair stalls, it was nearly time to go home. Katie's legs were getting tired and Daddy sat her on his shoulders, asking her if she had had a good birthday.

Tom was having a last look round and spotted a machine filled with small cuddly teddies and with a crane head hovering above. He looked at Katie and looked back at the teddies. She *loved* teddy bears and had a collection of nearly twenty at home, all shapes and sizes. Tom instantly wished that he had bothered to make a birthday card for Katie … but he knew she would *love* to have one of those teddies from that teddy-bear machine! It was 50p a turn. Tom checked his pockets for the chance of finding a 50p coin inside, but his pockets were empty. All of a sudden,

Tom felt very guilty for giving Katie just *one* piece of popcorn when he had eaten the rest, and he wished that he hadn't spent all of his two pounds, because then he might have had enough left to win one of those teddies for Katie.

Mummy called to Tom that it was time to go home, but as he turned around, a gush of Windy blew in his face, blowing his hat clear off his head, and along the grass! Tom was extremely annoyed at Windy, especially as he was feeling so bad at that moment. He stomped after his hat, shouting to Windy, 'I've had enough of your meanness, you naughty Windy! I think the whole world would be better off without you blowing around!'

Tom bent down to pick up his hat, and as he did so, he noticed something shiny in the grass. He leaned closer for a better look, and nearly fell over in shock when he saw what it was … There on the grass lay a perfect, shiny fifty-pence piece! It was just what he needed to win a teddy present for Katie! *Could it be possible that mean Windy actually has a good intention when she blows?* thought Tom suddenly. As quick as a flash he picked up the 50p and ran back to the teddy crane machine, shouting to Mummy and Daddy that he would be there in just one minute!

The Story of Windy

Tom had tried one of these machines before, and he remembered how difficult it was. But with nothing to lose, and everything to gain, he slipped the 50p into the slot and pushed the buttons controlling the crane. He steered the crane into position by pushing the lever. He nervously watched. He could not believe his luck when he saw that the crane had managed to grab hold of the leg of a cute little teddy! Tom held his breath and waited whilst the

crane slowly moved to the opening, and he could hardly contain his excitement when he saw the teddy tumbling down the exit chute! He picked it up carefully and, with a huge smile on his face, turned and ran to where Mummy, Daddy and Katie were waiting. He handed the teddy to Katie and said, 'Happy Birthday, Katie! I won this just for you!'

Katie was so happy with her little teddy that she couldn't stop smiling and hugging teddy tightly. 'Thank you Tom, thank you!' she said.

Tom was very pleased with himself and all his guilty feelings had disappeared. They walked back towards the car, with Windy blowing on their faces. Daddy was saying that maybe Windy *was* a bit mean sometimes, blowing air so cold that his ears nearly froze off! Tom stopped in his tracks, looked at Daddy and said, 'Oh no, Daddy, Windy is not mean at all! She wants us to know she's all around us if we need her … and she's telling you that you need to get yourself a warm hat, Daddy – that's all!'

Mummy, Daddy, Katie and Tom all burst out laughing, and Daddy said, 'How right you are, son! How right you are!'

… *And* as Sunny kisses Moony goodnight with her reflection, Moony says, 'Have a safe and peaceful day, Sunny,' to which Sunny replies, 'Have a safe and peaceful night, Moony.' And all the twinkling Starries glitter and giggle, 'Goodnight … goodnight.'

Windy

Does Windy try to be helpful with every blow she makes, do you think? Or does she just like to blow around randomly?

Could Windy possibly feel Tom's guilty feelings about Katie? Maybe that was why Windy helped him. . .

I wonder why Windy blew all the leaves off the tree? Did she do it for fun, or did she know that it was an important job that needed to be done? What do you think?

This is The Story of

Moony

Can Moony prove to be more help than Tiny Mouse could possibly imagine?

The Naturals

Once upon a time in a sleepy forest, Sunny fell down in the sky, and Windy's breezy blow lessened to a mere shivering of the leaves. The playful leaves danced happily, changing colour as they twisted this way and that. Silence fell, and in the distance Moony began to rise, shedding a welcome torchlight into the dense woods. 'I'll see you in the morning, Sunny!' called Moony through the treetops.

'Night, night, lovely Moony!' responded Sunny affectionately, as she continued to disappear under the horizon and bring a new morning to the world further west.

The birds nestled in their nests and the worms, spiders and insects blanketed themselves under the muddy leaves. The larger animals of the forest found their cosy lairs and the medium-sized animals crawled into their warm dens for a family cuddle before nodding off, safe and warm, to sleep.

A large family of thirteen mice were having a very hectic bedtime routine. Every evening before bed they had to brush their teeth and wash behind their ears. There was always a fight for the nearest leftover Rainy drops that Sunny hadn't yet dried up to wash themselves with.

The Story of Moony

Once they were all clean enough for bed, the scramble came for the best sleeping spots. Whichever way they all managed, Tiny Mouse, who was the smallest, always found herself sleeping nearest the entrance hole! One evening somebody suggested lying in a long line in age order, with oldest first. Of course, it was Tiny Mouse who was once again nearest the entrance hole. Another evening someone suggested that the strongest mouse should have the best spot, and so forth down the line. Of course, who ended up sleeping right next to the entrance hole? You guessed it – Tiny Mouse!

It wasn't so much that Tiny Mouse was uncomfortable sleeping there – she wasn't. Nor did she get too cold, because she was snugly squashed up against the next mouse in line, one of her brothers. It was because Moony was so bright, that Tiny Mouse felt it was daytime all night long, and never got a wink of sleep! The only time she slept was when lovely Cloudy covered the night sky. 'Thank you, Cloudy!' Tiny Mouse would say gratefully after one of those nights, and then she would stick out her tongue at Moony, 'Good Riddance, Moony! I hope I won't be seeing you again tonight!'

The Naturals

Tiny Mouse was also just a little bit afraid of sleeping so close to the forest beyond the entrance hole.

Moony was always smiling because he knew what was best for *all* the animals of the forest. Many animals loved the protective light of Moony and felt safe because

they knew he was watching over them. Some animals gave Moony not a single thought, and a few thought he was a big pain in the bottom – the way he purposely shone a light on their night-time hiding places!

One evening as Tiny Mouse took up her sleeping position by the entrance hole, she watched the others all fighting and scrambling together for their own sleeping spots. How she wished she was big and strong enough to join in the familiar night-time scuffle, with the yells and laughter that went with it. Instead, she quietly got herself comfy, and snuggled up to one brother 'duvet', jealously thinking that the rest of her family had a mouse duvet on *either* side of them. She could not see right to the far end of the sleeping line, where the last mouse there, too, had just one mouse duvet, just like her.

As silence slowly crept along the line, Tiny Mouse was comforted by the fact that Moony was being hidden by Cloudy that night. *Oh, goody!* she thought, *I'm going to have a good night's sleep and I'll be able to play all day long tomorrow, without stopping for a rest!* She settled down and drifted off to sleep.

The Naturals

After a while she was in the middle of her usual
dream, where she was scuffling amongst her family for a
sleeping spot, laughing and squealing with delight. In her
dreams she always managed to clamber over most of them
until she was about third or fourth in the sleeping line.
Having a brother and sister duvet on either side made her
feel very safe and cosy. There was another scuffle for the
final spots, and Tiny Mouse was getting pushed around by
her brothers and sisters; she was struggling hard, but this
time managed to squeeze herself into the second spot! She
was laughing and laughing in her dream – until it felt like
she was given one big push from
someone, which made her go
tumbling and tumbling
and tumbling! Over
and over and over
she went, doing
somersaults. She
felt as if she was
falling further and
further down,
until she was quite
giddy and bruised!

The Story of Moony

Tiny Mouse was asleep no more. She tried to open her eyes, but realised they already *were* open. *What's happening? Dreams cannot feel this real!* she thought, worried. Her wonderful dream had turned into a cold, dark nightmare.

She realised she was cold, and tried to feel around for her brother mouse. There was nothing next to her, and she was lying on sharp sticks and stones which were digging into her back. *This is definitely not my bed!* she thought. *I must have been accidentally kicked out of our hole and tumbled somewhere far, far away! Oh no! What am I to do? What am I to do?* Tiny Mouse squeaked with fright!

She had been told that whenever she was in a dangerous situation she had to stand as still as a statue until her family found her, but this was even more scary and dangerous because she couldn't see a thing around her! She knew it was extremely important for her to crawl into a hole, and not just *any* old hole that dangerous animals could be sleeping in! She realised that her family would not know she was missing until Sunny brought the morning with her. That may not be for hours and hours and hours!

Tiny Mouse couldn't move her leg, which hurt very much. She was beside herself with worry and didn't know where to turn *If only I had a bit of Moony now*, she thought sadly. *I wonder … maybe Moony would answer my wish if I pleaded hard enough. Anything's worth a try*, she decided.

'Dear Moony,' she started aloud, 'could I have some of your bright shining light? I realise now that you help show other animals the way when someone gets lost, and I could really use your help, please!'

Moony could feel Tiny Mouse's distress. He liked her words, but they were not necessary, for he was just about to help her anyway. He requested Windy's help to blow Cloudy away from his Moony light.

Windy sprang into action to blow away the large Cloudy, but of course at the same time, all the loose leaves surrounding Tiny Mouse stirred and began to tickle her body. Stray branches gently leaned in towards her, and Tiny Mouse felt light touches on her arms and legs. 'Oh no! What's happening now?' Tiny Mouse exclaimed in terror, 'What a time for Windy to start playing tricks on me! First Moony is against me, and now you, Windy!' she shouted. 'Please leave me alone!'

Of course, the faster Windy tried to blow Cloudy away, the stronger the leaves and branches flapped around Tiny Mouse, and the more the leaves and branches flapped, the more scared Tiny Mouse was feeling.

As Tiny Mouse realised there was nothing she could do but wait for morning to come, she tried to make herself relax. She knew she would have to save her energy to get through the night, and concentrated on the only things she could do, which was sniff the air, twitch her whiskers, and listen to the night-time noises.

The rustling of Windy's movements through the forest was strangely comforting to Tiny Mouse, as if Windy was hushing her softly. Even the gentle touches of the leaves and branches lost their scariness after a while. In fact, Tiny Mouse found she rather *liked* their touches now that she wasn't scared by them! They were just as comforting as her brother mouse duvet, in fact!

The Naturals

Tiny Mouse blinked for the umpteenth time. Only this time, she saw a bit of grey colour, instead of pitch black. She blinked again. Slowly she could make out the tree shapes surrounding her and, at last, she caught a glimpse of Moony. 'Oh, how wonderful it is to *see* you, Moony!' Tiny Mouse joyfully exclaimed. 'Thank you for coming to my rescue!' But she knew she was not out of the woods yet, not by any means. As her eyes slowly adjusted to the shadows and shapes around, she immediately searched for a nearby snug little hole she could pull herself into.

She quickly spotted a perfect sized cubbyhole and, looking all around for danger, she managed to crawl into it, dragging her hurting leg behind her. Once Tiny Mouse was safe inside, Windy blew over a bunch of leaves to surround her and her cubbyhole. 'Thank you, Moony, and thank you too, Windy!' Tiny Mouse whispered before snuggling under the leaves and falling, exhausted, to sleep.

'You're welcome, little one …' Moony's soft breath of a whisper was carried by Windy's faint breeze, and went unheard by Tiny Mouse's sleeping ears.

Moony's disappearance also went unnoticed by the sleeping Tiny Mouse. However, Tiny Mouse's disappearance certainly did not go unnoticed within the mouse household! 'Tiny! Tiny! Where are you? Where are you?' they all called the next morning, to no avail. A search party was set up and little groups of mice set off in different directions, calling for Tiny Mouse.

The Naturals

Tiny Mouse awoke to the realisation that she was still safe, although bruised, after having been helped by Moony. She peeped her little nose outside of her temporary cubbyhole and listened intently for the cries of her family. She knew they would search until they had found her, and she waited patiently.

Before too long she heard the frantic shouts of her family, and she signalled to them from her hiding place. 'I'm here! I'm here! Over here!' she cried. She was *very* relieved to have been found. They all admired her cubbyhole, thinking how very grown-up she had been to have kept herself safe. They took it in turns giving her a mousey-back ride back up the steep forest hill and into the safety of their own mouse hole.

They all made a great fuss of Tiny Mouse, and took wonderful care of her until her hurting leg healed. They made her laugh by jumping on top of each other, and scuffling all together so that it looked as if they were tied up in knots! They even pretended to push each other out of the entrance hole (as she had been), and returned back hopping on three legs, pretending to have hurt one!

The Story of Moony

Tiny Mouse thought this was hilarious and she laughed and laughed until her bruises ached!

When night-time came, someone suggested that Tiny Mouse should have the Number One sleeping spot, right down deep inside the hole, and everyone agreed. However, Tiny Mouse had no intention of giving up the best spot, which was at the end of the line, in full view, and under the safest, watchful eyes of … *Moony*!

... *And* as Sunny kisses Moony goodnight with her reflection, Moony says, 'Have a safe and peaceful day, Sunny,' to which Sunny replies, 'Have a safe and peaceful night, Moony.' And all the twinkling Starries glitter and giggle, 'Goodnight … goodnight.'

Moony

I wonder if Moony likes to annoy Tiny Mouse
by keeping her awake at night, or if he is just
concentrating on helping other animals
to see their way in the dark?

Do you think Tiny Mouse has learnt that even
though Moony kept her awake, his light was also
helping others who needed to see?

This is The Story of

Hailstones

Will Bull the Bully
learn his lesson ~ or will
Hailstone's aim backfire?

The Naturals

Once upon a time Rainy was hard at work minding his own business, and everyone else's too for that matter! He had just finished watering a few gardens, and some brightly coloured umbrellas – and a few bare heads! He could feel himself getting a little colder and stiffer and recognised the signs that he was about to freeze, so he called upon Sunny to throw a bit of heat his way.

'Sorry, Rainy!' Sunny shouted from a distance. 'I can't help you today, I'm too busy drying up a flood that you have caused elsewhere! I'll be there tomorrow, so meanwhile, mind you don't freeze!' Sunny laughed affectionately and turned away from Rainy to concentrate on her important job at hand. She laughed because she knew what happens when Rainy freezes …

Once in a while it just cannot be avoided that Hailstones show up and, like the hooligans they are, fall around causing noisy havoc everywhere, breaking everything in their path!

Hiding away inside Cloudy, Hailstones waited, not so patiently, to be called upon. They sometimes felt that they

spent all their lives waiting for a bit of the action (for the odd occasion when they could let rip and pound Earth, and anything that gets in their way). 'Move over, Rainy! It's our turn now!' they shouted. They were jingling around and itching to get started.

They had tried reasoning with Sunny and Rainy, saying that if they were needed more often, then maybe, just *maybe*, they would soften up a bit and cause less havoc. Sunny and Rainy said it was a nice idea and that they would think about it. However, they could not take that risk. After the last downfall of Hailstones, people were bumped on the head, ducks were banged on the back, buildings and cars were damaged, and gardens were ruined (with flower heads and petals strewn everywhere)! So Sunny and Rainy made sure that Hailstones only occurred rarely.

Everyone knows that Hailstones don't *mean* to be mean and hurtful. In fact, they do try to avoid knocking the heads and petals off *all* the flowers in someone's garden. They even knocked a burglar off his ladder once! They were very pleased with themselves, and after that decided to knock *everyone* who was up a ladder off it, just in case they were burglars too! Of course, most of them were window cleaners or people fixing their roofs!

The Story of Hailstones

'Oh well, never mind,' said Hailstones after that. 'People shouldn't be up a ladder when we're having a downfall – it's dangerous!'

Rainy had tried on several occasions to resist Hailstones' advances. He had shivered with all his might to keep warm enough to stay wet and not to turn to ice – but that didn't work. He had tried blowing onto his own Rainy drops with his own breath, but that didn't work either. Rainy had even huddled together as many Rainy drops as possible, to make one *big* drop that would not be as easy to freeze as a single little Rainy drop, only to find that it backfired in the worst possible way! Hailstones' bullets ended up being as big as apples shooting down from the sky! Well, you can just imagine what those devilish Hailstones got up to *that* day!

Needless to say, Rainy now knows there are some things one just has to give in to gracefully, and let all the Naturals do what they just have to do.

'Come along, freeze up, Rainy! You know you have to when Sunny's too far away. Oh, and thank you, Sunny!' shouted Hailstones. 'Stay away for as long as you can, please! And don't make us wait so long next time!'

Rainy had no choice but to harden and let Hailstones take over …

Once Hailstones had full control of the sky, they shouted, 'Hello, Earth! It's good to see you again! How good are you at catching us today, then?' They threw themselves into the air, and raced each other to see who was the very fastest Hailstone, that would touch Earth first.

When they landed with a thud, they all shouted, '*Me*! It was *me*! *I'm* the winner! No, you're not – *I am*! *I am*!' There was such a commotion, with all the Hailstones squabbling and bickering, 'I've won! I've won!' and then, '*You* haven't won! You've landed in a *tree*!'

'The rule was the first to touch *Earth*,' said one Hailstone. 'Yes, but the *tree* is touching Earth, and therefore so am I!' said the other, and so it went on, until they spotted one Hailstone being carried along on the top of a lady's hat – whereupon they all roared with laughter!

They were having such fun, until one of them spotted a lamb in a field who seemed to be looking very afraid. 'Hey, look everybody! Over there! Did any of you guys hurt that little lamb?'

'No! No!' they all said. 'We wouldn't hurt poor defenceless babies!'

'I can see what she's afraid of!' cried out one Hailstone. 'Over there! Can you see? It's a raging big bully of a bull! He's teasing the poor lamb by pretending to charge at her to make her run.'

'Yikes!' one Hailstone said. 'Even *I'd* be afraid of that!'

Most of the others agreed that they would be too.

'Come on, you guys, we're meant to be hard and strong!' another one of them said.

'Well, there's nothing we can do from down here, we're too far away – unless we call up to the others who are on their way down and tell them to aim for Bully the Bull!' one said.

'We shouldn't be *aiming* to hurt anyone at all – remember all those poor window cleaners we hurt? Or all those cars we broke last time? That wasn't good, was it? Plus they might accidentally land on the little lamb!' said another.

The Story of Hailstones

'We do try not to crash into things on purpose … sometimes!' admitted one. 'But that Bully the Bull needs to be taught a lesson.'

'Just because the bull is being a bully, it doesn't mean that we have to be bullies too! Right?' one asked.

'Quite right, quite right!' they agreed.

'I have an idea!' shouted one. 'Let's call for Windy's help to blow us over to the field. If we get ourselves in front of Bully the Bull, he won't be able to walk properly. He'll be wobbling all over the place with us under his feet, and he certainly won't be able to charge. Lamb can then escape!' he said.

'Brilliant idea!' they shouted. 'Yes, that's what we'll do!'

'Windy, Windy, show yourself! We need your help! Where are you?' they called.

'I'm right here!' Windy gushed. 'What mischief are you all up to, especially now that you're on Earth? I shall not be blowing you into *more* naughty mischief!'

'No, no, nothing like *that*, Windy! Where on Earth would you get a silly idea like that from? We want to *help* someone – and it has to be quickly! There's no time to explain. Please will you blow us to that field over there?'

Windy knew that Hailstones were mischief-makers, but she always believed in giving second chances. So she blew the little iced balls over towards the field. They rolled and rolled, over and over, crashing, bumping, rumbling and tumbling into each other.

The Story of Hailstones

'Wow, this is fun!' they shouted. 'We don't normally crash into each *other*! This is much more fun than smashing someone's kitchen window!

'Or landing in someone's hat!' piped up one Hailstone. They roared with laughter at the memory, although they became more serious as they neared the field.

The little lamb was indeed afraid for her life when she found herself wandering in the wrong field and came face to face with a bully of a bull! She didn't know what to do! She couldn't move her legs as they had turned to jelly. After what felt like a very long time staring at the bull, and the bull staring back (just waiting for her to run so he could charge), she heard a terrifying rumbling noise. She didn't know what was happening, but as long as the bull didn't move, she guessed she was safe.

The joint effort of all the Hailstones rumbling and tumbling towards Bully the Bull made them shiver with excitement. To have Windy behind them blowing them into position made them feel really rather special, and knowing they were about to come to the rescue of a poor defenceless lamb, well – that made them all feel *so* important!

After lots and lots of tumbling, they settled themselves into position, right in front of Bully the Bull. The large bull did not know what to make of all these hard white icy lumps, but it didn't put him off staring at the lamb. The lamb, however, was surprised at the icy balls near her legs and she jumped up in the air! This was all the movement Bully the Bull needed to get into a charging stance. He huffed and puffed and kicked one of his front legs forward a few times, knocking some Hailstones flying backwards, before lunging forward towards the lamb. She closed her eyes and feared the worst …

Hailstones braced themselves for action, and huddled tightly together. One of the bull's hard, muddy feet landed on a Hailstone – and squashed it flat! The second foot landed on top of another Hailstone, causing the bull to wobble a bit. The third foot landed on top of yet another Hailstone, causing the bull to lose his balance, and a hero Hailstone threw itself under the fourth foot, which caused the bull to topple over as if in slow motion, all four legs kicking at the air!

The Story of Hailstones

And do you know what the last thing was that a hundred Hailstones saw before they were squashed flat? *A great big hairy bottom!*

The lamb slowly opened her eyes and, to her amazement, Bully the Bull was sprawled out before her, unable to get himself up again. She watched for a while until she felt safe enough, then stuck her tongue out at the bull, turned around and trotted off, daintily treading between the funny iced balls with her little feet!

A big rumble of a cheer came from all the hero Hailstones. Whoops of delight followed whistles and shouts of, 'Hooray! We did it! We did it!'

'Let's give a large Hooray for the true Hailstone heroes of the day,' they cried, 'the ones under Bully the Bull's *bottom*!!'

'Hip, hip, hooray!' they cheered. 'Hip, hip, hooray!'

Rainy, Sunny and Windy were watching from the heavens, smiling down on Hailstones, who were, by now, happily melting into Earth.

... *And* as Sunny kisses Moony goodnight with her reflection, Moony says, 'Have a safe and peaceful day, Sunny,' to which Sunny replies, 'Have a safe and peaceful night, Moony.' And all the twinkling Starries glitter and giggle, 'Goodnight ... goodnight.'

Hailstones

Do you think Hailstones were worried about scaring the little lamb when they attacked Bull the Bully? . . . Or were they just thinking about saving her?

Even though Hailstones rescued the little lamb, do you think it seemed that they were also little bullies themselves?

Did you even believe that Hailstones were such big softies at heart?

This is The Story of

Sunny

Will 'hateful' Sunny be there
to rescue Little Mole when
he gets himself into trouble?

The Naturals

Once upon a time there lived a little mole. Now, Little Mole had a favourite game. It was to slide down the muddy bank just near his home. He preferred it when all his little brothers and sisters played his favourite game with him, but for some strange reason they didn't like to get all covered in mud as much as he did!

The muddier, the better! thought Little Mole to himself.

Each morning Little Mole would wake early and rush to the front door and look outside. If Rainy was out, Little Mole would yell, 'Yippee! Hello my friend Rainy! Muddy mud slide, here I come!' He would rush to eat his breakfast and ask who would like to play with him on the muddy bank.

The Story of Sunny

If, however, the glorious Sunny was shining, Little Mole would mutter and curse to himself. 'Oh bother! Not that horrible Sunny shining again, ruining my favourite game by hardening my muddy mud slide! I really hate that Sunny.' Sunny looked down upon Little Mole and smiled happily (even though Little Mole's words must have hurt her feelings).

One morning as he awoke, Little Mole was overjoyed to hear Rainy pounding against the front door. But to his disappointment, none of his brothers nor sisters wished to get all wet and muddy with him that day. Mother Mole had told them they would be going out for a walk in the forest later, and they didn't want to exhaust themselves too much in one day.

Little Mole asked Mother Mole if he could go outside and play his favourite game on the mud slide.

'Yes you may, Little Mole, but just for a short while as we shall all be going out for a nice walk later and I don't want you to be too tired.'

'Oh, I won't be! Thank you, Mother,' replied Little Mole, and off he skipped excitedly out into Rainy to play his favourite game.

As always, when Little Mole stepped outside into the shower of Rainy, it felt *so* good to wash off the caked-on mud that that naughty Sunny had hardened onto his fur, as well as ruining his favourite game!

The Story of Sunny

Little Mole was having such fun sliding down the long slippery slide and crawling back up again, over and over, that he wished he could stay and play all the time with Rainy. However, he had promised Mother he would be home soon. So after a while he skipped home again, washing himself clean in his lovely friend Rainy as he went. The house was all warm and cosy and Little Mole happily played with his brothers and sisters until lunchtime.

After lunch, just as Little Mole was beginning to feel rather tired, Mother Mole said, "Come along everyone, Rainy has stopped and it's time to go out for a nice long walk.'

Little Mole thought to himself, *Oh no! I feel far too sleepy to go out walking right now,* and he said, 'Mother, may I stay here at home please, where I am all warm and snug and cosy?'

'Oh no, Little Mole! We shall *all* be going for a walk this afternoon, and that's that!' replied Mother Mole sternly.

The Naturals

Little Mole knew it did no good to argue with dear Mother Mole, as she always knew best. Even so, Little Mole was feeling very grumpy indeed and didn't want to go out for a silly walk with everyone! Nevertheless, he set off with them, deciding to walk as slowly as he could so that next time Mother Mole might think it best for him to stay behind in their house, all snug and warm.

Little Mole was walking really slowly and he could hear that the rest of his family were a long way up ahead. He was day-dreaming about his favourite mud-slide game, and how it would now be in perfect condition for sliding down, after all the pouring Rainy had done this morning. He hoped that horrid Sunny stayed away, so as not to harden up all that delicious mud!

'Perhaps I had better catch up with the others and not be so grumpy, then maybe Mother will allow me to have another mud-slide game after dinner!' Little Mole said excitedly to himself. 'Yes, that's a good idea!'

The Story of Sunny

Just then he noticed a large puddle of water, and decided it would be fun to walk through it. However, the puddle was a lot deeper than Little Mole had imagined, and before he knew it, he was in the middle of the puddle and the water was right up to his neck!

Little Mole was all of a sudden very scared. He was standing on his tiptoes, and out of his depth! He started to shout to his mother and the rest of his family for help.

'Mother! Help me! Come back!' But, of course, Little Mole had trailed too far behind to be heard.

'Oh no! How I wish I had not walked so slowly, and that I was up far ahead with my mother and everyone right now!' he sobbed.

After a few minutes, Little Mole started to feel very cold because he was standing so still in the puddle, afraid to move. He was wondering how long he would be stuck in the puddle. How long before his family returned this way?

Or maybe they will return home another way! thought Little Mole with horror. *But surely they must realise I am missing? Then again, I was trailing behind on purpose, and they may just think I am only pretending to be missing!* Little Mole started to cry. He even began to wish that Rainy hadn't dropped so many Rainy drops that morning, after all!

The Story of Sunny

All of a sudden, Cloudy began to disappear and Sunny appeared, brightening up the forest and bringing colour to the leaves and flowers all around.

'Oh no! That's all I need now … that dreadful Sunny appearing and hardening up my favourite muddy mud slide!' complained Little Mole. But then he realised that unless he got out of this puddle, he might never be able to play on his mud slide ever again! Little Mole cried some more …

Meanwhile, Sunny was shining brighter and brighter, and Little Mole could feel his face becoming warmer and warmer. He was trying to be brave and keep very still so that he didn't topple over and fall face-first into the water! Someone *had* to rescue him soon. They just *had* to! Little Mole squinted his eyes against Sunny's bright rays.

'Oh, go away, you're hurting my eyes you silly, annoying, horrid Sunny! Help me somebody … help me!' Little Mole shouted, hoping that somebody could hear him. But Sunny just seemed to smile down upon Little Mole with her strong bright sunshine rays…

Just at that moment, Little Mole thought he felt the puddle of water becoming not quite so deep – as if the puddle was moving down from his neck to his shoulders!

That's funny ... thought Little Mole to himself, *I'm sure the puddle came right up to my chin a moment ago! It must just be my imagination. Water cannot disappear by magic!* But sure enough, the water was most certainly disappearing, right before Little Mole's very eyes! 'I just don't believe it!' shouted Little Mole excitedly. 'Hooray! Hooray!'

The Story of Sunny

Little Mole waited patiently in the deep puddle for the water to disappear down to his tummy, for he knew he could then wade safely back out again. He glanced up at Sunny smiling down on him and he realised that she was warming up his fur. Little Mole then had one *big* realisation – that it was *Sunny* who was drying up the puddle of water, so that he could be saved! And in exactly the same way that she dries up his muddy mud slide!

'Well, well! My goodness gracious me!' exclaimed Little Mole, feeling rather ashamed. 'You are *saving* me, Sunny, even though I have called you horrible names and said that I hated you! Thank you from the bottom of my heart … and I promise I will *always* be pleased to see you *anytime* you wish to smile down on me!'

Sunny continued to smile down at dear Little Mole, as he freed himself from the now not-so-deep puddle. He hurried away as fast as his little legs would carry him to catch up with the rest of his family, and to tell them all about the miracle of Sunny!

...And as Sunny kisses Moony goodnight with her reflection, Moony says, 'Have a safe and peaceful day, Sunny,' to which Sunny replies, 'Have a safe and peaceful night, Moony.' And all the twinkling Starries glitter and giggle, "Goodnight … goodnight.'

Sunny

Was Sunny annoyed that Little Mole got himself into a tricky situation, or was she, nonetheless, just happy to do her best to help?

When Little Mole was making 'hateful' remarks to Sunny, do you think Sunny felt upset by them? Or do you think she was only pleased to be saving Little Mole?

This is The Story of

Rainbow

Will Rainbow have to take
drastic measures to help Sam
find her treasure?

The Naturals

Once upon a time on a cold dark night, Sam was getting ready to go out when he would normally have been getting ready for bed. He was so excited as he stepped outside the front door, and all his sleepiness disappeared as cold Windy blew into his face.

As Sam and his family bundled into the car, he looked up at the sky to the twinkling Starries and made this wish: 'Starry, please can I see Rainbow?' Whenever Sam saw a Starry, he always had the same wish. He had seen Rainbow in books and on posters, on walls and on the television. But *never* had he seen one for himself up in the sky. He didn't actually believe Rainbow existed, although he knew Mum and Dad wouldn't tell him tales.

The Story of Rainbow

Starry heard Sam's wish and made a mental note to tell Rainbow all about Sam when he next saw her on the horizon.

Sam didn't know where his family were taking him. It was to be a surprise and he loved surprises! He was told he had to wrap up warm, and Mum made hot chocolate milk in a flask, which she packed in a bag with some biscuits.

It must be a midnight picnic under the stars! thought Sam. *Wow – that would be so cool!*

His family knew how much Sam liked to look at anything that twinkled, shone and glittered. His eyesight was not too good and many things looked blurred to Sam, but anything shiny, and especially full of colour, Sam could see just as well as you and I.

As Sam's eyesight was fading, his hearing was improving. He could hear the tiniest scratching noises coming from inside a kitchen cupboard that no one else could hear. Mum said she'd rather *not* have known they had a mouse in the house at all, but admitted that it was a good job really, so they could catch it and put it safely in the field, before they ended up with hundreds of baby mice running all over the house!

Sam was the best at playing hide 'n' seek around the house. Or rather, he was the world's best *seeker*. He could hear the faintest rustle of a shirt, or the tiniest scratch of a shoe, and would point and shout, 'Found you! Found you!'

Their car eventually came to a stop and they all got out. 'Keep a hold of our hands, Sam,' said Mum. 'This way, everybody!'

They headed up a grassy hill, and joined a crowd of people all walking in the same direction. Sam could make out an orangey-red glow in between the shadows of the people but couldn't figure out what it was exactly, until he heard loud crackling noises and caught the waft of smoke up his nose! As they made their way right to the front, dodging past other people, Sam could feel the heat of the most enormous bonfire he had ever seen in his entire life!

Sam was entranced with the dancing flames reaching high up into the black sky. His face was feeling warmer and warmer until he hid himself behind Dad and felt the chill of the cold air. He blinked in the dark shadow of Dad for a few seconds, before standing in front of him again to feel the strong heat on his face, and the strong light in his eyes. 'What's the matter, son? Don't you like it?' asked Dad.

'Oh, I like it very much, Dad. In fact, I *love* it!' declared Sam, 'I've never been so hot and so cold so quickly, nor has it ever been so light and so dark so quickly either! Well, apart from when I shine a torch into my face and turn it off and on, off and on,' he explained.

Having the time of his life, and enjoying the strong sensations, Sam jumped behind Dad again. Then he jumped in front of Dad. Behind Dad, in front of Dad. Behind Dad, in front of Dad. Heat off, heat on. Light off, light on. 'Steady on, Sam,' laughed Dad, 'or you'll make us all giddy in a minute!'

'Sorry Dad! But this is really cool! Well, not when I'm in *front* of you, then it's really *hot*!' said Sam, laughing at his own joke. Just then they heard a loud bang.

The Naturals

'Come along, Sam, over here!' shouted Mum.

'Fireworks!' shouted Sam, even louder. 'WOW! My favourite! I *love* fireworks!'

Sam's eyes adjusted to the black sky, and he could make out the glittery sparks that looked liked Starries, the difference being that the glittery sparks quickly disappeared, unlike Starries who hang around for ever.

As Sam was watching the firework display in the night sky in wonderment, he knew that he would keep it in his mind's eye always. He watched in awe as a rocket zoomed across the sky before banging into a fire-crackling purple shower. He closely studied the green and red sparkles intermingling with each other high above, and listened to the fizzy whistling sounds of the spinning Catherine wheel. With silver sparks flying off it in all directions, people had to move hurriedly away!

At one point the sky was filled with such amazing colour and the noisiest bangs, that Sam thought the whole *world* must be able to see and hear it! He felt that he was in the centre of Earth, and only imagined that heaven felt

The Story of Rainbow

like this, too. *Rainbow must be heaven's firework*, he thought, *along with the bangs and claps of thunder as her back-up rock group!* He giggled to himself at the thought.

There were gasps from all the people watching, and clapping and shouting, and Sam could hear shouts of, 'Look over there!' and 'Look at that one!' and 'Wow! That's a good one!'

When the last BANG had echoed through the skies, and the final shower of coloured sparkles was swallowed up by the dark night, Sam and his family huddled together on a blanket drinking hot chocolate and eating biscuits. They were sitting near enough to the bonfire to be kept warm, but not so near that they turned into toasted marshmallows! Then Sam got a piggy-back ride from Dad back to the car.

Back at home, Sam was asleep before his head hit the pillow, but not before removing his glasses, and saying a sleepy, 'Goodnight Mum, goodnight Dad – thanks for a wonderful night that I'll always treasure! It was the very next best thing to seeing the real Rainbow …'

The next day was dark and Cloudy, but Sam didn't mind. He spent the whole day in bed resting his eyes and reliving in his mind's eye the brightness and colour that he had seen last night. Before he went to sleep again that night, Cloudy had gone and so he searched for Starry in the sky and said, 'It wasn't quite Rainbow, but I did get to see a sky filled with colour! So thank you, for *sort of* making my wish come true, Starry.'

Starry listened. Rainbow was ready and waiting for Sunny and Rainy to clash together, before she could show her colours to Sam, but they were both busy doing important jobs around the world.

Washing, drying, washing, drying — that's all they do all the time, Rainbow thought impatiently. She knew how important it was to show herself to Sam before his eyesight grew too weak for him to see her. She decided to think hard to hatch a plan which would help Sam's wish come true …

The next day Rainbow had rather a naughty idea. She asked Windy for her help, and Windy blew on the remains of the bonfire that Sam had seen the other night. It had been put out, but Windy's breeze fanned alive some smouldering embers hidden deep inside the ashes. Bits of paper and sticks blew onto it, and before long, a second bonfire had appeared. 'Are you sure we're doing the right thing, Rainbow?' Windy called. 'This looks a bit dangerous to me …'

'Trust me, Windy,' said Rainbow. Windy blew and blew, and the fire grew and grew …

The Story of Rainbow

'Rainy, Rainy!' called Rainbow ever so slyly. 'A fire! Your help is needed, come quickly!' Rainy was soon to the rescue, showering down on top of the bonfire that was newly sprung to life.

'A showering is not good enough,' offered Rainbow, 'you need to *pour*. More Rainy … more … more …'

After a while Rainy said, 'That must have done the trick, Rainbow!'

'No, not yet,' Rainbow said. 'I can still see some red sparks!' So Rainy poured and poured, and he poured some more.

Meanwhile, Rainbow mischievously called to Sunny that Rainy was making a flood, and told her that her help was urgently needed! Sunny appeared and immediately said, 'That's enough, Rainy! You can stop now whilst I dry your Rainy drops up again!'

Well, this was all the intermingling of Rainy and
Sunny that Rainbow needed to show herself off! In full
glorious colour, and in perfect order of red, orange,
yellow, green, blue, indigo and violet, Rainbow came to
life and filled the sky. She looked towards Sam's bedroom
window and had another idea – to give Sam something to
treasure *for ever*.

She made her Rainbow's end shine straight into Sam's
room, and fill it with brilliant, brilliant colour! Sam didn't
know *what* was happening! He thought his eyes had gone
to heaven to find Rainbow for themselves! When he
looked out of the window, he realised that Rainbow had
found her own way to him on Earth! She had given him
her treasure which he would keep in his mind's eye and
remember for ever.

The Story of Rainbow

... *And* as Sunny kisses Moony goodnight with her reflection, Moony says, 'Have a safe and peaceful day, Sunny,' to which Sunny replies, 'Have a safe and peaceful night, Moony.' And all the twinkling Starries glitter and giggle, 'Goodnight ... goodnight.'

Rainbow

Even though Rainbow was quite sneaky about
getting Sunny and Rainy together,
do you think this was okay, because, after all,
Rainbow did have good intentions?

Did Rainbow do something naughty when she
asked Windy to blow the ashes to make a fire?

Do you think it mattered to Rainbow that Sam
was grateful to her?

This is The Story of

Rainy

Does Rainy make things
worse for Little Piglet. . . or
can he truly save the day?

The Naturals

Once upon a time there was a little piglet who had a lovely dirty pigsty in which to roll around. He lived with lots of other pigs and piglets who seemed to be utterly happy living in the dirty pigsty. However, Little Piglet just could *not* understand how they could be so happy being so dirty, so crusty, and so smelly … YUK!

Whenever Little Piglet could sneak away from the smelly pigsty, he did. He would wander over to a nearby meadow which was covered with sweet-smelling grass, and even sweeter smelling flowers. Here he enjoyed rolling around in the grass to try and wipe away some of the crusty mud from his pink skin. He also enjoyed the freedom of not always bumping into the other pigs back in the sty. For some reason, all his pig friends seemed to enjoy huddling up together, treading on one another's

trotters, and having their noses a bit too near each other's dirty bottoms! YUK – *smelly*!

Now, Little Piglet had a friend, a cat called Mirabel. They had first met in the meadow and Little Piglet envied her so. Her coat of fur always looked so clean compared with his muddy body. He had then found out her secret of licking herself clean, and thought this was a splendid idea – but his tongue wasn't as rough as hers, and his 'fur' was more like bristly whiskers than her soft velvety coat. However much he tried to lick, he could never get himself *really* clean – and it tasted awful as well!

One day Mirabel invited Little Piglet to her party to celebrate the fact that she hadn't yet lost any of her nine lives. She lived across the meadow, and Little Piglet had been looking forward to Mirabel's party for days. He wondered who her other friends were, and if they were all as clean as Mirabel! Perhaps there would be different types of animals there, too. Then maybe Little Piglet could see if there were other ways one could wash oneself. He was getting extremely excited at the thought of finding out!

The day of the party arrived and Little Piglet was very excited. He awoke early and ate his breakfast, being careful not to slop the food all around his face. He then rubbed himself up and down against a fence to scratch off some mud he had on his back. Next, he wandered around in the grass to try and unstick the muddy bits wedged in between his trotters, before lying down on the clean grass and rolling over and over, to rub himself as clean as he possibly could.

Sunny was climbing higher in the sky, and Little Piglet decided it was time to set off across the meadow to Mirabel's home. On the other side of the meadow he came to a field, and he could see the farm where Mirabel lived. He ducked under the fence and started to trot across the field. He was about halfway across when he heard a distant thudding trot – which quickly became not so distant!

Little Piglet let out a squeal, and gathered up speed before looking over his shoulder in the direction of the frightening noise. The animal chasing him looked as scary as it sounded! It was a big brown cow, and Little Piglet had obviously chosen *his* field to walk across! Not a good idea! But it was too late to do anything about it now.

The Story of Rainy

Instead, Little Piglet trotted as fast as he could, all the time fixing his eyes on the waiting fence in the distance.

Because Little Piglet's eyes were set upon the nearing fence, he was not looking where his trotters were treading. Suddenly he tripped and somersaulted head-over-heels into some soft, squidgy muddy stuff that smelled awful! Now, as you know, Little Piglet was not particularly fond of mud – but this was *not* mud – this was *cow poo*! YUK!

Little Piglet's top priority was to reach the fence, so up onto his legs he rolled and, still squealing, he once more attempted to trot as fast as he could, to get to the other side of the field. He could no longer hear the cow chasing him, but he was certainly not going to turn around and look again!

Little Piglet reached the fence and flung himself underneath! Safe at last, he looked around for the cow, but it was nowhere to be seen.

Poor Little Piglet was by now the dirtiest he had ever been in his life, and there was no way he could even bear to put his tongue into the nasty, smelly cow pat and lick it off! It was already beginning to harden, just like mud, onto his whiskery coat that a moment ago was as clean as it could be.

How could he possibly go to Mirabel's party looking (and smelling) like he did? Poor Little Piglet was *so* upset on his way to the party, when he should have been all happy and excited.

The Story of Rainy

As if to sympathise with Little Piglet's mood, the sky became darker. He then felt some very cold drops of water on his back. *Oh no! Now I shall catch a cold, as well as being dirty and smelly!* he thought miserably.

None of the pigs in the pigsty liked being outdoors whenever Rainy was about. They always headed straight back into the sty at the slightest drip of Rainy! Little Piglet had always followed the others under cover because they said it wasn't nice for pigs to get wet, and that one always starts to sneeze and shiver afterwards.

So here was Little Piglet, dirtier than he had ever been in his whole life, having been chased by a scary cow and fallen head first into a very smelly cow pat, and on top of everything he was going to catch a cold! He couldn't go to Mirabel's party now … he just *couldn't*! Little Piglet was also more upset than he had ever been in his whole life before!

He turned round and started to follow the fence around the field, making his way back home again. He certainly was *not* going to crawl under the fence like he had before, and meet that scary cow again!

Rainy's drops were tickling Little Piglet's body as they slid downwards and plopped off onto the grass beneath his trotters. Little Piglet realised he quite *liked* the feeling of Rainy on his skin. Rainy was not making him shiver, as the other pigs had said, Rainy was *tickling* him, and he liked it very much! He sadly watched Rainy's drops falling to the grass by his trotters and noticed how dark and dirty they were. 'That's strange,' muttered Little Piglet to himself, 'I didn't think Rainy's drops were *that* colour! I thought they were clear.'

Little Piglet stopped walking to study Rainy's drops more carefully. He couldn't understand how they fell from the sky one colour, and fell onto the ground *another* colour. He stood quite still trying to work out this mystery. 'What on Earth could make Rainy's clean drops look so dirty, I wonder?' he questioned out loud.

Little Piglet slowly realised that he was no longer feeling quite so dirty. At about the same time, he realised that it was only those raindrops dripping from his *body* that looked dirty, and *not* the ones falling to the ground, straight from the sky.

The Story of Rainy

Little Piglet began to feel a little flutter of excitement in his tummy which grew and grew, as he realised this meant that Rainy was washing him *clean* – and that maybe he *could* continue on to Mirabel's party after all!

He lifted up his legs one at a time to be cleaned by Rainy, and then he decided to do something he had never done before, which was to lie right down on his back on the muddy ground, to allow Rainy to shower all over his tummy, and in between his toes. Then, standing up again, he got into all sorts of funny positions so that every inch of his hard fur could be reached and cleaned by Rainy.

Little Piglet was one extremely happy pig as he resumed his walk to his friend Mirabel's party. From being dirtier than he had ever been in his whole life, he was now the cleanest, shiniest, most sparkling that he had ever been in his whole life!

When he arrived at Mirabel's party, Rainy had stopped, and Little Piglet was positively glowing with clean radiance – and there was not a single sneeze in sight! Little Piglet was so proud of himself. With a huge grin spread across his face, he wished Mirabel congratulations, and said hello to all of her friends.

'I'm *so* pleased you are here, Little Piglet! We thought Rainy might have stopped you from coming,' said a rather worried Mirabel.

'Oh no, certainly not!' replied Little Piglet. 'Most certainly not!' And he happily reminded himself that from now on, he had his very own special way of keeping himself clean, with his new friend, Rainy!

... *And* as Sunny kisses Moony goodnight with her reflection, Moony says, 'Have a safe and peaceful day, Sunny,' to which Sunny replies, 'Have a safe and peaceful night, Moony.' And all the twinkling Starries glitter and giggle, 'Goodnight … goodnight.'

Rainy

Do you think Rainy just wanted to wash Little Piglet, or do you think he wanted to show Little Piglet that he could be helpful?

Do you think Little Piglet felt wise when he realised by himself that Rainy is not bad for him, like the other pigs had said?

Do you think that Rainy is even wiser than Little Piglet?

This is The Story of

Starry

How does Starry help Gracie make someone's wish come true?

Once upon a time, when all was quiet and dark inside Gracie's bedroom, a small beam of light found a gap in the curtains and danced around Gracie's sleeping face.

With a start, Gracie rubbed her eyes and yawned. She was just about to jump out of bed to start getting ready for school, when she realised that it wasn't Sunny telling her the day was beginning. It was just a silly little Starry trying to wake her up, *and* it was still night-time!

The Story of Starry

With a sigh, Gracie walked over to the window and peered through the curtains. She studied all the twinkling Starries, trying to figure out which one had woken her. There was one extra bright glittering Starry in the dark sky who was twinkling merrily away, and Gracie had her eye on him for a while.

'Okay, which one of you guys woke me up? Was it you, Glitter Starry?' she asked, looking at the twinkling Starry. 'You look a bit cheeky to me. What's it like being a Starry? I wish *I* could be a Starry one day.' Then she hopped back into bed and fell sound asleep.

That night she had a dream. She dreamed that she had joined all the Starries in the night sky. They were not quiet and sleepy at all, as Gracie had suspected. They were giggly and mischievous and were looking forward to a whole night-time of fun! They were jiggling around and trying to bump into each other. They never managed to, but they had fun trying.

Glitter Starry was absolutely the most mischievous Starry. The one who had woken her up, in fact. So over she flew to meet him eye to eye, to tell him off …

'What do you think you're up to? Glittering away as if you're the crown jewels, and purposely shining in my face to wake me up!' she scolded him.

'Oh!' giggled Glitter Starry. 'It was such fun watching you sleeping … ha ha ha! You make such funny faces … hee, hee, hee! Did you know that you snore?' he asked cheekily.

The Story of Starry

'Oh, no I don't! I do *not* snore!' shouted Gracie.

'Well, how would *you* know?' retorted Glitter Starry. 'You wouldn't know because you're asleep! Anyway, now that you're not asleep, follow me and let's have some fun!'

Gracie was no longer angry with Glitter Starry for waking her up. She was much more interested in finding out who all the other Starries were, and what they got up to at night. She wondered if they were all as naughty and mischievous as Glitter Starry, or if he was the worst! As she looked closely at them, she could see that they all had individual smiley faces – and personalities to match. They were so friendly, and funnily enough they all knew her name, and giggled 'hello' as she flew by!

Gracie felt very at home with her Starry friends, and looked around for Glitter Starry. She heard him shout, 'Here I am, Gracie! Over here!' Then he hopped out from behind another Starry. 'Look, I can make myself invisible!' he said, and promptly disappeared again, by hiding behind yet another Starry!

'We Starries do like playing hide 'n' seek with each other,' he continued, 'but we really like hiding from Moony because he is just soooooo nosey. He likes to know what we are up to and watches us all the time! And when Moony isn't watching us, then Sunny takes over and reports back to him!' Starry groaned.

'Well, they must both care about you a lot,' stated Gracie. 'So that's nice …'

'Well, I just call it *nosey*!' declared Glitter Starry.

All of a sudden a strong but gentle voice said, 'I suppose you're talking about me again, dear little Starry?'

'Oh! Yes, Moony, in actual fact I am,' confessed Starry. 'How come you always hear what I'm saying? You must have *very* big ears!'

'It's probably due to the fact that you never whisper, dearest Starry,' said Moony, chuckling to himself. 'And you must be Gracie. It's a pleasure to meet you, Gracie.'

The Story of Starry

'Why, thank you, Mister Moony!' Gracie said, thinking she should be bowing or something. 'I've never seen you this close before, and you're very … BIG!'

'Thank you, Gracie,' said Moony, 'and so are you – you must be eight now …'

'Yes, that's right, I am,' Gracie said proudly. Moony smiled and went on his way.

'Wow!' exclaimed Gracie, 'I can't believe I've actually *spoken* to Moony!'

'Well, it's funny you haven't spoken to him before,' said Starry, 'because millions of people on Earth speak to Moony every night!'

'Come closer, Gracie, and see what else I can do!' exclaimed Glitter Starry. 'Hold on tight to me – we're going for a flying sliding ride around the Milky Way! Have you heard of the Milky Way before, Gracie?

'Oh yes,' replied Gracie. 'They taste deliciooooouuuuuusssss!'

The Story of Starry

Before she could finish her sentence, Gracie had been whisked off with Glitter Starry on the most magical roller-coaster ride of her entire life! They were propelled away faster than the speed of light, shooting this way and that way, in and out of the Starries making up the galaxy that is the Milky Way, and round and round the planets! Up and down, and from side to side they went. The roller-coaster ride seemed never-ending. Indeed, Gracie felt she could have stayed on that magical ride forever … without even getting dizzy!

They then slowed right down to about a thousand miles an hour. Gracie's breath caught in her throat at what she saw. There were flashes of colour so magnificent, it was as if she had walked into a paint shop, and all the paint was being thrown up into the air all at the same time! Flashes of colour surrounded her, far more beautiful than the most beautiful firework display she had ever seen! 'That's the making of Rainbow!' Glitter Starry giggled.

They quickly slowed down, and then stopped completely. 'Wow! That was just *fantastic*!' whooped Gracie with such joy!

'That's not the best part of being a Starry,' Glitter Starry proudly announced.

'What on Earth could beat that?' wondered Gracie.

'Look closely up at Earth,' suggested Glitter Starry,' and tell me what you see.'

'Well, for a start, I'm looking *down* at Earth, not *up* at her!' offered Gracie, stating the obvious.

'Ah – that means nothing, Gracie! Turn upside down like me!' Glitter Starry told her. 'Now, look closely *up* at Earth and tell me what you see.'

As Gracie studied Earth, really focused on her, she began to see more and more. It was as if she were holding a magically powerful telescope. The picture before her eyes became deeper and deeper, bringing her vision closer and closer to something important, Gracie could feel. Then, all of a sudden, she was face to face with a little boy who was wishing upon a Starry! She felt very honoured, and a bit embarrassed to be listening in on a stranger's secret wish. As if she was doing something impolite – rude even. But

The Story of Starry

she listened to every word as if her life depended on it.
The boy said:

'Dear Starry, I know you have many more important
wishes to grant, but here is my wish … please can you tell
my best friend, who is up there with you, "Glitter One …
Glitter Two, I won't forget you!" Thank you, from George
… Oh, and if he could get a message back to me, that
would be *really* cool!'

The magical 'telescope' zoomed backwards as Gracie's view returned to the night sky and the multitude of happy, giggling Starries. Gracie turned to Glitter Starry and said, 'Wow! Did you hear that, Glitter Starry? Did you hear George's wish?'

'No, Gracie, I didn't,' replied Glitter Starry. 'He was talking to *you* …'

'But *I* can't make wishes come true!' hollered Gracie.

'You'll find a way, Gracie,' was all Glitter Starry would say. 'You'll find a way …' Gracie could not believe that Glitter Starry had made her responsible for making someone's secret wish come true! It was definitely not fair of Starry to make her do something she could never possibly manage to do!

'You'll find a way, you'll find a way …' were the words that kept repeating inside Gracie's head when she awoke next morning. For a minute she wondered where she was. She couldn't remember leaving Glitter Starry and coming back down to Earth. Then she realised with relief that, of course, it was only a dream!

The Story of Starry

'What a wonderful dream!' Gracie said aloud to herself. 'Apart from the bit about that boy and his wish ...' She remembered very clearly what George had said. 'As it was only a dream, I'll just forget all about it!' she said to herself. 'Yes, that's what I'll do, I can forget all about George's wish. After all, there's nothing I can do about it, anyway.' With a clear conscience, and with joy in her heart, she leapt out of bed for another day of school.

As Gracie was leaving for school, Mum reminded her that they would be popping in to visit their next-door neighbour when she got home. A boy called Ray used to live next door. Gracie hadn't seen him for a while, when Mum told her that he had gone to heaven.

Gracie then had the funniest feeling – she felt that she had been with Ray not so long ago. But that couldn't be! 'Hang on a minute,' she said to herself. 'Ray reminds me of Glitter Starry from my dream!' The more she thought about Glitter Starry, the more she realised how similar he and Ray were! *It can't be ... it couldn't possibly be!* Gracie kept thinking.

She couldn't shake off the idea all day, and didn't quite know what to make of it all. Should she be spooked? She didn't really feel spooked. She felt special, in a spooky sort of way! It was definitely a very special dream she had had last night!

After school, when Gracie was back at home, Mum got ready to go with her to Ray's house. Gracie put on her coat and wanted to tell Mum about her dream and the feeling about Ray, but the moment passed and she kept quiet. *It must just be a coincidence*, she argued with herself. The fact that Ray once shone a torch from his bedroom window through the gap in her curtains to wake her up, like Glitter Starry did, was just one *big* coincidence! One *HUGE* coincidence …

Gracie had decided she wouldn't mention any of this to her mum, and especially not to Ray's mum as it might upset her. Until … they walked through their neighbour's front door and Ray's mum said, 'Hello Gracie, I'd like you to meet George, he was Ray's best friend …'

The Story of Starry

Well, Gracie was too gobsmacked to speak, let alone move! There, standing in front of her, was the face she had seen and heard in her dream!

'Say hello, Gracie,' said her mum. 'Gracie?'

Gracie did not say 'Hello'. Instead, she said, 'Glitter One, Glitter Two, I won't forget you!'

While Mum was trying to understand what Gracie was saying, and why she was saying it, George jumped up and down, shouting, 'Yes! A sign! A sign! Well done, Ray – Yippee!' Meanwhile, Ray's mother was asking Gracie how on *Earth* she had known George and Ray's secret code for each other …

Gracie explained her whole dream story, and Ray's mum then explained how, when they were younger, she had found both boys covered from head to toe in glitter, and had called them 'Glitter One' and 'Glitter Two' for a whole month! She knew it had still been their secret code-name for each other.

There was such joy and happiness in Ray's house that afternoon. Gracie felt very honoured and special to have been a part of it – 'special' in a spooky sort of way, mind you. She was so pleased that she had told her dream story, and especially that she hadn't ignored George's wish upon Starry, after all!

... And as Sunny kisses Moony goodnight with her reflection, Moony says, 'Have a safe and peaceful day, Sunny,' to which Sunny replies, 'Have a safe and peaceful night, Moony.' And all the twinkling Starries glitter and giggle, 'Goodnight ... goodnight.'

Starry

When Starry told Gracie that Earth isn't
upside~down, was he trying to show her that she
only has to turn her own view around,
to see things more clearly?

I wonder how Moony and all the Starries knew
who Gracie was. . . Could it be because
they look after her each night?

Was it a good thing that Gracie told her dream to
everyone? Surely it would have been easier for her
not to have told her dream to anyone?

What would you have done?

This is The Story of

Earth

Does Earth manage to keep the ticklish foot~roots of all the seedlings snuggled firmly underground?

The Naturals

Once upon a time there was a flower in bloom. Not just any old flower, but a soon-to-be Mother Flower. Feeling very heavy, and expectantly anticipating the dropping of her baby seeds, Mother Flower nodded silently in Windy's breath. Her heavy head drooped so low that she nearly caught it in her outstretched leafy arms. She was looking forward to watching her baby seeds nurture and grow. There were lots of gaps in Earth around her in preparation for the new arrivals.

It wasn't long before the Sunny days were shortening. The still-warm puffs of Windy gave Mother Flower a wonderful swinging ride, and she was caught gently by her flower friends who were swaying around too. 'Not long to go now!' they would say whenever their flower heads touched. 'If you have to wait much longer, you'll be so heavy, you'll be *bowing*!'

'I know, I know … and oh, I can hardly wait to hear the pitter-patter of my seeds dropping down to Earth!' replied Mother Flower excitedly.

The Story of Earth

Meanwhile, the baby seeds were able to chatter away to each other. Half of them were feeling nervous about their forthcoming task of growing up into decent-sized flowers, like Mother. The other half were excitedly looking forward to the challenge of flower life, and maybe even growing taller than Mother. Not all of them, however, were looking forward to the long, long, long drop down to Earth. 'It looks a pretty long way down to me!' muttered one seed warily.

'I can't make it, I can't make it! She can't make me do it!' said one very scared seed.

'Of course you can make it! It looks easy-peasy to me,' offered a more confident seed.

'When the time comes, let's just close our eyes and imagine we're falling into chocolate cake! The gardener says it looks just like Earth, only more delicious,' advised another seed.

'Well, I'll be *diving* down!' said a seed with a bit of a daredevil streak in him. 'I won't just be falling or dropping down, and I won't be aiming straight for Earth either!' he said. 'I'm going to bounce off that flower over there, then jump over that gate, before hopping on to that big stone and catapulting into that splendid spot of Earth right over there!'

'Wow! That sounds thrilling!' said a seed in astonishment. 'How brave you are!'

'You seem to have that all planned nicely,' said another. 'Good luck. I'm just going to float down to whichever spot I find myself in.' And so it went on ...

Finally the day came when Windy was having one of her *very* Windy days, and Mother Flower couldn't hold on to her baby seeds any longer. 'Goodbye babies!' she called. 'I'll be right here keeping my eye on you for as long as I can. Be gooooooood ...'

The Story of Earth

Her voice faded up into the distance as the sibling seeds were blown further and further down. Earth was at the ready, and with dark outstretched arms that mingled in with the rest of her colour, she was ready to greet the babes. One by one they plopped into Earth's cosy warmth and fidgeted around a bit to get really comfy. After all, they would have to remain in the same position for a very long time.

'Wow! That was a soft landing!' many seeds shouted.

'That was *fantastic*!' said the seed who was really scared before. 'I could do it all over again!'

'What became of the daredevil?' someone asked. 'Where is he?'

'Oh, I think that may be him over there, sitting on top of the fence,' one said. 'Hey, Daredevil! Are you stuck up there?'

'No, of course not! I'm taking a break and enjoying the view. I'll *blow off* later … ha ha ha!' quipped the daring seed. All the seeds giggled at Daredevil's smelly remark.

'I think *I'm stuck*,' said a soft little voice. 'I said, I think *I'm stuck*!' it called again, louder.

'Who's stuck? Where are you?' shouted the seeds.

'I'm up here! I'm wedged into the wall! Please help me!' the little seed pleaded.

The seeds studied the cracks in the old stone wall, looking further and further up, until there, near the top, they spotted her. She couldn't move. She couldn't even jiggle around. Little Seed was well and truly stuck!

The seeds chattered worriedly together, 'What shall we do? What on Earth shall we do? Mother, Mother, can you hear us?' they called up to Mother Flower. Mother Flower looked down smiling at her seeds. She could not hear them calling. She could not see Little Seed stuck fast in the old stone wall.

Earth, however, had heard their distress and was trying to figure out a plan to save Little Seed, who was caught up high.

'Windy!' Earth said. 'Windy! Please help Little Seed by blowing her off the wall and down to me!'

'I'll do my best for you, Earth,' said Windy, 'but keep a good hold of the other seeds or I may accidentally blow them *all* into the wall!'

'I'm holding them tight,' said Earth, squeezing herself tightly around the seeds in her care. 'Go ahead and blow, Windy.' Windy huffed and puffed and blew hard at the wall to try and dislodge Little Seed. But, if anything, she only succeeded in pushing Little Seed back even further into her hiding hole!

'It's no use,' said Earth. 'We'll have to think of something else.'

'Wow!' shouted Daredevil from his perfectly chosen Earth spot. 'How did you get up there, Little Seed? I wish *I'd* thought of that spot deep inside the wall. That was a brave manoeuvre!'

'I have an idea!' Windy shouted to Earth. 'If we can't get Little Seed down to you, then let's get *you* up to Little Seed! She'll be sheltered and snug enough through the cold winter months, Rainy will be able to seep through the cracks in the wall to reach her, and come springtime, Sunny will lure her out once she starts growing.' She continued, 'We just need *you* up there, Earth, to keep her warm and to encourage her foot roots to grow!'

'Okay, Windy – let's do it!' Earth encouragingly exclaimed.

So Windy blew again; from down low to up high, she blew and she blew. Soft bits of Earth flew over towards the wall.

The Story of Earth

'Hold on tight!' the seeds said to each other. 'You can do it, Windy! Nearly there! Just a bit more!' they shouted, and then, 'Yes! You did it, Windy! Well done, Earth, for flying so high!'

'That was a cool stunt!' Daredevil seed called out to Earth.

There were enough bits of Earth to cover Little Seed cosily in her new home, but not before Little Seed had managed to shout a big, 'Thank you, everybody! See you in the springtime!'

'Come along now, the rest of you lovely seeds,' said Earth, 'you must be exhausted after all that excitement. Snuggle down inside me for a good long rest, and we'll talk again when spring is here. It won't be too long ...'

Sure enough, after what seemed like a big blink of an eye, hard Earth was being thawed by Sunny's rays. The cold, moist, muddy Earth was soon replaced with warm, moist, muddy Earth, which was then turning to warm, dry, *not*-so-muddy Earth.

The seeds were all beginning to wake up. They wanted to have a good stretch and do something, but they weren't sure what to do, or even how to do it.

Sunny made the days longer, and Earth had to call out to Rainy for a drink. 'Come down, Rainy, we need you!' she called. 'The seeds are itching to get moving and explore outside their shells.'

Windy excitedly intervened. 'I'll help! I'll help!' she called, and she blew Cloudy over in front of Sunny.

'Do you have Rainy in there with you, Cloudy?' asked Earth.

'I'm here for you, Earth – are you ready for a good soaking?' asked Rainy.

'Just a good *sprinkling* for now, please, Rainy,' replied Earth, 'we wouldn't want to flood the poor seeds away – they're nearly ready to sprout!'

'Here we go then!' laughed Rainy, and he enthusiastically showered his Rainy drops all over Earth.

The Story of Earth

The budding seedlings were waiting with anticipation under Earth. They knew they would all become flowers one day, but they weren't sure exactly *how* it would happen. They started to buzz excitedly as they felt Rainy's drops gently tickle their bodies. 'Ooooh, that feels nice!' one seed said, and the others all agreed.

'What if my toes tickle when they touch Earth, and I don't like it?' asked a seed.

'Maybe you *will* like it,' suggested another.

'But I don't think I will – I think I'll grow very sensitive foot roots,' he said.

'Well, then, we'll find you some "Daisy Roots" for your feet. I heard the gardener say they were the best things for feet,' the other seed suggested helpfully.

'How will I know which way is the right way up?' the seed worried some more. 'What if my head ends up down in Earth, and my leg roots end up kicking about in the sky?'

The Naturals

'Well, then, we'll all end up laughing at your wriggly legs!' giggled the other seed. All the seeds jiggled about, laughing at the thought.

'Just remember,' suggested the helpful seed, 'you need a hot head and cold feet. Your head should grow towards Sunny and your foot roots should grow further and further into dark, cold Earth. Now, repeat after me,' he continued, 'hot head, cold feet. Hot head, cold feet …'

The Story of Earth

Before long, all of the seed siblings and, in fact every one of the dropped seeds around the garden, all waiting patiently under Earth, were chanting to themselves, 'Hot head, cold feet. Hot head, cold feet. Hot head, cold feet,' just in case there came a crucial moment when they needed to remember.

After some time one seedling excitedly shouted, 'I think something's happening to me!'

'Me too!' they all chorused.

Sure enough, as night turns to day and as day turns to night, all the seeds started to sprout. Arm shoots with little heads on the end were drawn out from their shells, and unfurled themselves towards Sunny. At the same time, little foot roots stretched downwards, snuggling themselves further into warm, cosy Earth.

The Naturals

'Hello there! Hello there!' the seedlings joyously cried, as many heads protruded up through Earth – and there was not a kicking leg root in sight!

'There's Mother!' cried one, 'Hello, Mother, hello, Mother!' they all shouted together.

'Hello, my darlings!' said a tearful Mother Flower. 'I'm *so* happy to see you all again!'

'It won't be long before we are all as tall as Mother!' they said to each other. 'Let's have a competition to see who can grow into the tallest flower!'

'Yes, let's do that! they shouted.

'Where's Little Seed?' remembered one seedling, and they all looked up to the old stone wall.

They could not believe what they saw, for there, growing out from the wall, was the most beautiful budding flower they had ever seen! 'Hello everybody!' she said. 'I've been waiting for you to come out to play!'

The Story of Earth

'But how can that be?' they asked. 'How come you are so big when *we* are all still so tiny?'

Mother Flower explained, 'It's because she has been kept extra warm and snug by the old stone wall, and didn't get as much frost on her as the rest of you did.'

'*And* because she's so much nearer to Sunny up there than we are down here!' piped up one seedling. 'Isn't that right, Mother?' Everybody laughed, and Mother Flower said, 'Why, yes, little one! You must be right.'

All the seedlings cheered loudly up at Little Seed, because she had, in fact won the competition already, by being the tallest budding flower out of all of them! She was actually already taller than Mother Flower, and she still had a whole lot of growing to do!

... *And* as Sunny kisses Moony goodnight with her reflection, Moony says, 'Have a safe and peaceful day, Sunny,' to which Sunny replies, 'Have a safe and peaceful night, Moony.' And all the twinkling Starries glitter and giggle, 'Goodnight … goodnight.'

Earth

I wonder why Little Seed was blown apart from her brothers and sisters? Could it perhaps be to show her that things can still turn out good, even when they look hopeless?

I wonder why Windy's efforts at trying to blow Little Seed down from the wall, didn't work?

Perhaps even Windy knows things that look bad, can turn out to be not so bad, after all ~ and even she has to try to figure out another way forward sometimes. . .